Tall Grass
and
Buttercups

and Other Stories

Novello Nightingale

ISBN 978-1-9996129-0-0

Published by
Llyfrau Cambria Books, Wales, United Kingdom.
*Cambria Books is a division of
Cambria Publishing.*
Discover our other books at: www.cambriabooks.co.uk

Cover design by Carolyn Michel

For

Anne,Tessa, Lin, Cath and Judy

The Stories

To Joan,

love

Cynthia

Tall Grass and Buttercups

She had left guilt at the cottage gate, slipped it off like a snake's skin, of no further use. Now there was the solace of the bottles in her pocket, and from time to time she let her hands caress their smoothness, their promise.

The tractor grooves in the lane were baked hard and she walked clumsily over the ruts, catching now and then the scent of the hedgerow, remembering picnics in the fields when the children were young, egg and cress sandwiches, lemonade, tired babies slumped in her arms.

She reached a gate in the hedge, but the grass in the field was thin and nettled, in the corner a few sheep grazed. So not here then, not here.

The day seemed darker, fear slotted itself slyly into the space guilt had left, putting hesitation where there had been determination.

In the next field young calves grazed, lifted heads to stare.

She had never been fond of animals, never drooled over lambs or kittens. Or babies, though she supposed she had loved her own. Difficult to remember them as children, as adults they were sharp, defined. Janet, living in France with her two boys, coming home rarely, the children confusing her with their rapid French. And Adrian with his posh friends and a lifestyle she could only guess at, sending money but not coming himself because he couldn't stand Harry.

The rough walk was tiring but gradually the quietness of the lane blurred the edges of her uneasy mind.

When the grandchildren came they didn't want to walk anywhere, mooched sullenly in the garden or attempted tennis on the old court, took themselves off to town when they couldn't stand Harry any more.

'Why on earth did you marry again?' Janet asked.

'Because it's my life' she said, 'it's my life'.

1

The day was slipping away, she felt time dribbling through her fingers. At the next gate she rested her hands on the bar and looked over. The grass was long, there were no animals, it was just what she wanted. There were some early buttercups too, and that was a bonus. The children used to pick great armfuls of them on their way home from Sunday School. They would dump them on the kitchen table and she would fit the untidy stems into jam-jars. All week the windowsills would be golden with petals and pollen.

It was a high gate and padlocked, she looked down at her hands, twisted, arthritic hands, the knuckles swollen, and felt a sudden compassion for them, for all the work they had done, for the tears they had dried, the other hands they had held in love and pity.

Not fair to end like this, she thought.

Harry's hands were slender, almost dainty, she hated to see him messing up his food with them. Once he came in from the garden and presented her with a handful of crushed snails.

For the first time she had put him into respite care, had left notes for the children and the solicitor. Tidying a life away.

She felt she couldn't go any further, she would have to climb the gate. It was difficult, her hands couldn't grip properly, and for a moment she balanced wildly on the top rung. Then she was over. She walked to where the grass was long and thick, the flowers welcoming, and sat down.

Briefly she remembered another field and a man who wasn't Harry.

Now she took a bottle of water from her pocket and made a little nest in the grass to steady it. Then the two small bottles.

With childproof caps.

She took a deep breath, she'd opened them before, she could do it now, but her hands were hot and sweaty, time and time again she tried, got confused, was it twist and press down or press down and twist?

She sat back down, told herself to stay calm, stop shaking, stop shaking.

Then she was hot with rage, rage at her hands that after all the

2

years of service they should choose this moment to let her down, she found a stone, bashed at the bottles, the thick plastic resisted, wasn't even dented.

Desperation fuelled her anger and she used the stone on her hands until horrified by the bleeding she cradled them under her arms.

For a while she stood, gaunt, unlovely among the flowers. Now there was the gate to be climbed, the long lane. And Harry.

It was still her life.

Lollipops

Her laughter followed him down the drive, it seemed to linger in the car as he crawled through the early morning traffic. Georges' mind groped for a word to describe it. Maggie had never been a laughing woman, not even a smiling one, in Georges' eyes she was more of a whiner, a nagger, much given to slamming dishes in the sink, always on the edge of some vast irritation.

So why the laughter? There was only one word for it, it had been joyous and Maggie and joyous laughter was too incongruous to imagine.

Seeking some sort of explanation, he went over the events of the night before...after their meal he had taken the dog for a walk while Maggie did the dishes and was back in time to watch a particular programme that was a must on Tuesdays. Then there was that finance series that he always hoped would tell him how to get rich, the news, the bedtime cocoa, precisely at ten thirty he was between the sheets.

True he usually got up about four o'clock to go to the bathroom, but he was very quiet about it, pausing only to tweak back the bedroom curtains and look out at the garden.

George had been an avid reader of science fiction in his youth and some sneaky part of his mind still believed in UFO's and aliens landing. His fantasy was that when they came it would be in his garden. He thought of them as large round flat lollipops with stick legs. They wouldn't have features but would conceal intelligence far beyond that of mans. He pictured them slowly coming towards him and passing through the walls.

He got back into bed and his wife heaved herself over taking most of the duvet with her.

Her half-snore, half-groan conveyed to him in familiar matrimonial shorthand that a) he had woken her up, b) now she'd never get to sleep again and c) who did he think he was going to see in the garden, leprechauns?

Seven o 'clock on the dot he was at the breakfast table and about to put the third spoonful of cereal into his mouth when across the table from him Maggie pushed back her chair.

'George' she said, 'I think we have come to the parting of the ways. I'm leaving you'.

A solitary cornflake detached itself from the rest and slipped down his unprepared throat, the resulting choking fit had been spectacular, Maggie he felt had thumped him unnecessarily hard on his back. It was after he had wiped his eyes and drunk some orange juice that she had begun to laugh, that joyous, ringing laughter.

He was still rattled when he slid into his parking space at the office. Unbelievingly he was five minutes late, a fact the general office couldn't let pass.

'Can't have this George, never been known before, out on the tiles last night?'

Their banter followed him into his office where the phone immediately rang, Maggie's voice…

'I meant it'.

'What, what….' He stammered, but the phone was dead.

Angrily he dialled his home number then Maggie's mobile but there was no answer.

Nothing went very well that day, though he kept telling himself he shouldn't be worried, she had probably gone shopping.

As soon as he put his key in the lock he knew the house was empty. The kitchen, the living room were just as he had left them that morning, Maggie's chair was pushed back from the table, she hadn't even put the lid on the marmalade. A sudden thought made him dash upstairs, but no, she wasn't sprawled across the duvet, a neat bullet hole in her head, there were no splashes of blood in the shower. One thing he did find though, her clothes and makeup and jewellery were gone.

So she had left him. Back in the kitchen he looked with distaste at the dirty dishes. Rummaging in the fridge he found some ham and a tomato. It was Wednesday, he should be having lamb chops, veg, gravy.

Why hadn't she left a note? That bald statement at breakfast wasn't enough to dissolve nearly fifteen years of marriage, look what a good husband he'd been, a model if ever there was one. He took his ham sandwich into the living room and switched on the television. Then he found the Dear John note. Maggie had put it where she knew he would find it, taped to the remote control.

George, she had written, this is the happiest day of my life, perhaps I should be grateful to you after all one cannot know bliss if one hasn't known despair, and how I've despaired over you George. Have you any conception how boring, how mind-boggling boring you are? Everything done at the same time, in a certain way, same meals on the same days, same programmes on the telly, same holidays with your equally boring brother and his wife. I know I should never have allowed it to happen so in expiation for my guilt I'm not asking you for anything.

All I have taken is half the money in our joint account, I have done with security and pension plans and all the stultifying predictability of our life. I have no plans, no security, and that's the way I want it. Maggie.

She must be mad, off her trolley, bonkers! It couldn't be true that she didn't want anything, didn't want him! He'd always worked hard, well probably it wasn't the right description, but he'd looked to the future, saved, there was the prospect of a pretty good pension. What she called boring he called being sensible.

George sat and fumed till he realised he was watching the nine o-clock news, his sandwich curling drily on the plate. He searched out a bottle of whisky, poured out a cautious drop and added water. He realised that if he didn't clear up the kitchen then nobody would. The weak whisky wasn't doing very much so he had a drop more, without water. Then another. For the first time in his life George was drunk. About four o'clock he staggered out of bed. Coming back from the bathroom he looked out of the bedroom window.

The garden was full of lollipops and they were coming for him.

Thomson

Thomson Thompson, one with a p and one without, understood he was in deep trouble, in fact he'd probably have to kill himself.

What he didn't understand was how it had happened, he couldn't recall a bump, a yelp, yet there in the road behind his car was the furry heap his mother-in-law called her dear little Diddums.

It didn't move, and he was too scared to touch it. Calamity had struck just when his relations with his in-laws had begun to thaw somewhat. Not a lot but enough to give him hope that one day they would look at him without sighing.

He considered his demise, nothing involving knives or blood, Maria wouldn't put up with the mess, pills perhaps, or jump off a cliff, but this was Lincolnshire, nothing more than two feet high. He pictured himself trailing round chemists buying tablets, then the fuss of swallowing them, he'd be sick, he knew he would.

Thomson opened the gate and staggered as far as the lawn at the side of the in-law's house, he sat on the grass and leaned on the faux marble statue of Venus, or somebody like that. No arms anyway.

He waited for the screams, the beating of breasts, the blows raining on his head. Maria would do that, she could be violent at times, and she was as besotted with Diddums as her mother.

Nothing. No sound from the house, perhaps he could just get away with this, drive off, come back and join in with the weeping? It was a private lane leading to the side of their house, dead end too, so all he had to do was back out and get away before anyone saw him. Simple.

Carefully he edged the car back, using the grass verge and got out to make sure he hadn't disturbed the corpse. Realised his tyre marks were visible in the mud. He scrabbled with his feet to get rid of them, tore some leaves off the hedge and scattered them over the marks. It wasn't very successful, Morse would be on to it like a shot. Thomson wondered about DNA, what had he touched? The gate of course, he rummaged in the glove box and found a duster, still encrusted with last year's windscreen flies, rubbed anxiously at the gate, wondered where else he had touched, thought of the statue, had he touched that? It was all too much, he'd have to go over that as well. He felt faint, anxiously he used the duster on the legs, steadying himself by clutching it around the waist.

Voices then and from the back of the house came Mother and Father-in-Law. With dear little Diddums.

Everything froze, Mother-in-law spoke first, and Thomson could swear ice dropped from her lips and splintered on the gravel.

'What are you doing Thomson'?

'What are you doing Thomson' echoed Maria, coming through the gate, 'your car is blocking the lane, I couldn't get past.'

It was easier to answer Maria.

'Thought I'd have a bit of exercise, jog up, leave the car down there.'

'Some jog, its all of ten yards, what are you doing with the statue?'.

'It had some bird mess on the legs, thought I'd wipe it off, just trying to be helpful'.

Carefully he folded the duster into a neat square. 'I'll just put this back in the car'.

'Well, watch out for that big cat from the farm, it's sitting in the middle of the road, I booted it off, but it'll probably be back, get itself killed one of these days.

Father-in-law went slowly back into the house, you have an only daughter, love her, care for her, endlessly finance her and then she marries a Thomson.

He needed a drink.

On the Train

Apparently, there's a special bus laid on, so when you get off the train it takes you right there and that's a great relief, I'm hopeless at finding places, the map in my head is permanently upside down. It's not the sort of place you'd want to ask directions to either, at least everyone on the bus will be in the same boat, and if that sounds silly, well, I know what I mean.

I don't want to chat with anyone, I'm not prepared to go that far, well, they'll hardly be the crème-de-la-crème, will they? No, I shall avoid eye contact and if I am drawn into a conversation then I'll be pleasant but distant like the vicar's wife was when she came to say how sorry she was for our little spot of bother. Dolly said it was nice of her, but she didn't see the collection box waved under my nose.

You'll have guessed it's my first visit, I thought it best to let him settle down, but today's his birthday so I'm making the effort. I made him a little cake, just a fairy cake really, but there's icing on top and Dolly put in a little file she got in a Christmas cracker, just as a joke. Do they have bars on their cells now?

There's quite a lot of people on the train, woman over there reading a book, kids running around being a nuisance, she's not taking any notice. People shouldn't have kids if they can't control them.

Not that I shall say anything, she might get a contract out on me or something, no, keep your head down girl, pretend you're on the Orient Express, old Poirot will be along soon.

Bit of rain splashing the windows, I've finished my paper, there's no trolley so I can't get a cup of tea, quite a way to go still.

To think I could have been in Majorca, Kevin promised me that holiday, he always was a good-natured boy, I told the judge that, never been in any trouble, always good to his Mam, just easily led that's all. Trouble is, they see all that metal on their faces, studs and rings and things and the tattoos and they're prejudiced before they hear the

9

evidence.

Four years he got, it's too much out of a lad's life, I think they get remission for behaving but Kev's a bit hasty with his fists, like his Dad, that's if Jack is his Dad, I was never certain but if it was the insurance bloke then he was ever so mild-mannered. No use worrying over it now.

I've a pretty good idea what it'll be like when I get there, if television is anything to go by you sit in a place like a canteen, only there isn't any food, just tea in paper cups and the prisoners wear little red pinny's, our Kev'll die if he has to wear one of those.

I'm not going to go on about the holiday, he'd have done it if he could, it was just bad luck leaving his mobile behind in the bank, careless really, I expect he only took it in the first place so he could ring that Sharon, mustn't tell him she's going out with his mate now. He can do a lot better for himself.

I said that to our Dolly, but she started on about how I couldn't run his life for him, as if he's doing any better himself.

We had quite a little shouting match, me and Doll, till the cat jumped off my lap and even the gold fish looked a bit scared.

I worry about that goldfish, nothing to do, nowhere to go, I bought a little plastic tree and put it in the bowl, but it doesn't seem interested. Sometimes when the cat's gone walkabout I put the bowl on the little table in front of the telly and flick through the channels, but nothing takes its fancy though it seems to sulk when Ant and Dec are on.

Just a couple of stops now, there's butterflies in my tummy. Though knowing my luck they're probably moths.

More rain hitting the windows, good job I put the little cake in a plastic bag and I did remember my umbrella.

Posh woman across the aisle from me, can't think she'll be going to the same place. Lovely suit and you can always tell expensive shoes, can't you?

I'm not looking forward to getting off this train, getting on that bus, mixing with….them.

We're coming into the station, people herding up their children, the woman in the suit is standing up too. For a moment our eyes meet, and I see the same look I saw in my mirror this morning, part defiance, part desperation. She looks away.

I put on my coat and pick up the little cake. I don't want to get off this train, I positively ache to stay on it, go anywhere except where I'm going. It's a small open station and I can see the bus waiting.

While I was on the train I could have been anyone, going away for the day, visiting friends, once I step on that bus I'm branded, marked.

But there'll be no eye contact, no conversation, I'm determined about that.

They came early

They came early, as they always did, bursting through the door, shrugging off coats and scarves, hugging and kissing and Merry Christmasing.

Come in, she said, come in to the warm. They exclaimed at the tree, admired the lights. Oh, she said, it's a bit lopsided, I didn't know whether to cut off that bottom branch. It's lovely Mabel, you worry too much, it's lovely.

Uncle Percy poured the sherry and Phoebe, fat as ever, wedged herself into the only chair that would hold her. From the sofa Mum and Dad raised their glasses. It wasn't long before the two boys raced upstairs to the spare room where the old train set was laid out, but little Molly clung tightly and followed her like a shadow.

The house filled with the scent of tangerines and roasting turkey. Sometimes she thought it was the smell of Christmas she loved best of all on this day of loving and laughing. This day that redeemed all the other days. As always, Jack carved the turkey, a flowery apron around his waist, and George poured the wine. She told them the story of how the turkey was too big to carry, she had to have a taxi home and how nice the driver was, carrying it right into the kitchen for her. After a good tip, I bet, said Percy, but no, he didn't want anything. And as for the chestnut stuffing well they were so scarce this year she despaired of getting any and then she spotted some in the market, and she had the last ones and she thought they'd be all bad but no, there was hardly any waste at all.

It was all the best ever, they declared, they'd looked forward to this all year and she was doing them proud.

They pulled the crackers, read out the silly mottoes and wore the paper hats, red and purple and green. Was the dinner alright? She asked anxiously, and they assured her it had been wonderful, and she was to go and sit down and chat to Mum and Dad while they did the

12

dishes.

It'll take you all tomorrow to find anything, her Mother said, but it didn't matter, she'd sort it. Then it was present time and soon the room was awash with paper and bows, the children threw streamers, young Molly was persuaded into a new dress someone had given her, everything was chaos, and everyone was laughing. She would remember the laughter, hug it close in the lonely days.

They tucked into dates and crystallised orange and lemon slices, played silly games, arguing over the rules and sank exhausted to wait for tea. Couldn't eat another thing, they all said, but somehow the trifle and sandwiches and cake all went. She apologised for the cake, she couldn't manage the icing now her fingers were so arthritic. Oh, stop fretting, Mabel, Percy said, the cake was super, absolutely super.

Too soon it was time for them to go, they crowded into the hall, shrugging into coats, finding gloves and scarves. Percy pranced around with Phoebe's hat on his head and his hand on his hip.

Over the babble she called out, see you all next year!

Their voices died away, it was her mother who took her hand.

Next year Mabel, you'll be with us.

The door closed behind them, slowly she went back into the sitting room, the immaculate sitting room, with the bottle of sherry and the solitary glass. For a moment, a thin quiver of panic went through her. Then she thought, that tree is lopsided, and reached down and switched off the lights.

Tea on a Tray

At night the bedroom closes around me, compacts itself so that the darkness oppresses, flattens me further into the bed. A thin new moon links the curtains where they don't quite meet, the intricacies of rufflette something Gran has never quite sorted.

Beyond the curtains and that sliver of moon there's space, relentlessly unending, unfathomable, and I wonder in my sleepless nights, if that's all there is, then where's heaven, our Father which art in? I feel a particular interest in where it is, given the circumstances.

Never thought about it before, life was Uni, friends, music, laughter. Everything in front of me. So, I'm expecting a lot from heaven. I'm owed.

Pain threatens, the first mild twinges, I try to relax, ride it out, my hands clench.

Gran comes in, I must have cried out, she holds my hand, but I want to be held, I ache for arms around me, but she's the wrong generation, she can't bring herself to hold me. We always hugged, me and my friends, love you, love you.

I sleep for a bit and then the nurse comes, and I'm washed, the bed changed, injections injected.

Gran has picked some sweet-peas, the scent mocks me, brings memories that I don't want, Dad's garden, pick the flowers love, don't let them go to seed.

Gran brings someone upstairs. 'The Reverend has come to see you' she says, he comes in and Gran wipes the seat of the chair.

I see his lips twitch, he's youngish, suited, not the jeans and tee-shirt type, I can imagine his congregation drooling over him. I give him ten out of ten for his bedside manner.

He picks up the book I'm trying to read, talks easily, very likeable.

Gran comes in with two mugs of tea, she's slopped them a bit

14

coming up the stairs. The mugs are thick, and I gesture towards the dying plant on the windowsill, he takes the hint and pours the tea away. He is about my age, but whole, healthy.

I wait for him to offer a prayer, but he takes my hand, kisses my cheek, says he'll pop in tomorrow if that's alright. Then he's away for a bit at other parishes, they don't just have one church, they have to spread themselves nowadays.

I'm half asleep the next afternoon, a bit drugged, I think they've stepped up the medication, perhaps I should be grateful, but it makes the room hazy. I hear the doorbell go, but no-one come upstairs for a bit.

Then Gran comes in, she's discarded her apron, there are beads around her neck. Behind her the Reverend. He's carrying a tray, I glimpse china, matching china, delicate, white with a thin gold line.

Gran pulls over the little table, the one the nurses use, she takes the chair and he sits on the side of my bed.

I wonder how he's squared Gran about this but square her he has. She crooks her fingers over the fragile cup as if tea with a man of the cloth happens every day. There's little sweet biscuits too, and I try to manage one, but the tea is wonderful. He holds the saucer for me, I need two hands for the cup.

Then Mrs Brown from over the road comes charging up the stairs, I can see Gran is quite pleased to have a witness to our little ceremony, especially one of Mrs Brown's gossiping stature. She trots downstairs for another cup and more hot water. I wait for the inevitable mug to appear but it's a cup and saucer from her wedding china, I'd never seen it out of the cabinet before, must be the influence of the holy one. I wonder if she's washed it.

Before he goes, he kisses my cheek again, murmurs something I'm too tired to catch, a prayer?

In the night I float into space, drifting beyond the curtains, still trying to fathom the unfathomable, still looking for heaven.

Angie's back bedroom

Old Harry's gone, he was ninety-two and he died in his sleep so there weren't too many tears shed.

True, his sister in Swansea made some sobbing sounds over the telephone when she was told but as she hadn't seen him in thirty years we didn't take it too seriously. She said she was much too frail to come to the funeral, she was saving her strength for a month in Tenerife and did Mam know if Harry still had the Waterford glasses that Aunty May left and should by rights be hers?

She rang the next day to ask when the will was being read, well Mam and Angie had a good laugh about that, old Harry had just about enough insurance to pay for his funeral, that's if we didn't have brass handles on the coffin. Most of his pension went down the drain at the Red Lion except for the bit he gave Angie for his board and lodge.

As soon as he was packed off to the funeral home Angie put a notice in the paper-shop window saying, Room to let, suit pensioner, must be tidy.

It wasn't there half an hour when a thin young woman with three small children knocked the door and said she'd take it. Angie explained it was a small room and she only wanted a pensioner, but the woman became abusive and said she was being victimised. She changed her tune when Angie's son Terry came to the door; Terry plays half back for the rugby team and gets a certain amount of respect in the village. So, the woman and her kids moved off but not before the eldest had kicked the fishing gnome into the little pond Angie has in her front garden. He pulled it out though when Terry held him upside down over the pond.

There was a good crowd for the funeral, you can always get a day of for a burying round here, and afterwards we all crowded into Angie's cottage for the usual baked meats, everyone pitched in with something, Mam took a big plate of Welsh cakes and they all went even the burnt ones she hid in the bottom.

Then it was down to the Red Lion and fair play, Betty and Tom had put some things on the counter for us, crisps and sausage rolls, Scotch eggs, doyleys on the plates too. Someone put a plastic daffodil on the chair Old Harry usually sat on and from time to time we raised our glasses to it. It wasn't long before the singing started, Bread of Heaven, Myfanwy, Come back to Sorrento, we weren't choosy. Round about midnight things started to get a bit silly, and if you're wondering how we came to be there after closing time, well, our local copper was the one collecting glasses, that's when he wasn't doing his impression of Bet Lynch wearing beer mats for earrings. In fact, he was the one who started the conga, down the street we all went, round the crisp factory, past the church, and back along the canal bank, which was a bit risky. When we got back to the pub Betty and Tom had locked up and gone to bed.

Angie soon got another pensioner for the back bedroom, seemed a quiet little man, the woman who brought him said she didn't have room now her daughter was expecting again. He came down to the Red Lion sometimes, drank tomato juice, not a drink much favoured by us.

Angie worked part-time for Jones the Fish, down at the chip shop, which was handy for us, she always gave good portions, there was much shuffling in the queue so that we reached the counter when it was her turn to serve.

This particular Friday night, Angie was helping Jones to cut up some cod, when the knife slipped, and she gave herself a nasty gash, there was blood everywhere, some of it went into the curry sauce, but that was alright after a good stir. Now Angie was a large woman, well able to take care of herself, but she habitually fainted at the sight of blood, so rather than having her sliding into the chip fat, Jones reluctantly said she could go home. He rang Terry at the rugby club and the pallid Angie was duly collected.

They cut across the field and went up the back path, noting their lodger's window was open and the light on. Before they entered the house, they heard distinctly amorous noises coming from the room.

17

Angie was all for storming upstairs, but Terry made her wait and they sat in the little kitchen in the dark.

After a while they heard the bedroom door open and with much giggling on the landing there were eventually footsteps on the stairs. Terry put on the light, and to his and Angie's astonishment it was a total stranger escorting a mini-skirted blonde. Apparently, their mild little lodger had been renting out his room to the local lotharios when Angie had been doing her stint in the chip shop. Terry had never seen Angie so angry, she sent the lodger packing but not before she had made him pay for a new bed.

After that she didn't let the room to pensioners, she took in a girl from the council offices and now on the nights Angie works, Terry doesn't go down the rugby club, he keeps the girl company in Angie's little back bedroom.

The Golden Day

It was to be Thomson's golden day, a Sunday he would have all to himself. Maria was having a weekend at a Spa and though normally Mother-in-law would have insisted he went there for a meal they were having important guests and Thomson didn't quite fit into that category.

Maria had left him a list of chores, so he'd spent all Saturday mowing the lawn, weeding the flowerbeds, tidying the shed, picking up her dry-cleaning. Gladly, happily he'd worked, determined to have Sunday free.

He rather fancied a full English for breakfast, but Maria never bought bacon, so he contented himself with two fried eggs, fried bread, beans and sausages he'd bought when he picked up the dry-cleaning. He carefully erased any traces of the meal and put the rest of the sausages in the boot of his car to dispose of on the way to work.

Cunningly he shook up the muesli carton and put it back in not quite the right place.

Maria had left cold chicken and salad for his lunch, but Thomson had other ideas, colleagues had mentioned the superb steak-and-ale-pie served at The Feathers on Sundays, so he'd booked himself in. It was near enough for him to stroll there, even have a pint, no need for the car. He'd have to dispose of some of the chicken and salad along with the sausages.

Thomson was so smug it almost hurt, he gathered up the Sunday papers, put the lounger on the immaculate lawn and settled down. Utter bliss. The sun was quite hot, after a while he went in for a cold drink and his old baseball cap and was on his way back when the phone rang.

Mother-in-law.

'Thomson, I want you to do something for me, Percy was tidying the garden and he stepped on the rake so I'm taking him to Casualty, his foot's swelling up and its really painful, well, you know we're having guests tonight and I've made a casserole in advance, its already in the oven and it can't come out till half past twelve, so I need you to come over and take it out for me, you know how long it takes in Casualty, I can't be sure I'll be back in time.'

It was the longest speech Mother-in-law had ever had with Thomson. It could be worse he thought, he'd have time to do it and still be back at the Feathers for lunch, and it may earn him a few brownie points from Maria. He had time for another spell on the lounger.

His dry mouth woke him, he stumbled into the kitchen for a drink, glanced at the clock, saw the time....five past eleven. Perhaps he'd have a shower, freshen up, strapping on his watch he thought the battery must have gone, it said ten past one. So did the bedroom clock, and the one in the kitchen. Thomson realised it must have been five to one not five past eleven when he checked.

Panic stations then, he grabbed his car keys, raced to the car, remembered the in-law's keys, raced back again and finally swerved out of the drive.

As he opened their kitchen door the smell hit him, he yanked open the oven door and reeled back from the acrid smoke. Mother-in-law had put the oven gloves handy, he pulled out the casserole. Disaster of the first order, he couldn't get the lid off at all, it was welded to the base. He almost broke a knife getting the two separated. He buried his face in his hands, beyond weeping.

A car went past, he hoped it wasn't the in-laws, he needed time, time. He could at least try to reduce the damage. He found a basin, started picking off the burnt bits. There were a lot of burnt bits, in fact more burnt bits than what was left. Inspired he tipped out the contents into a saucepan and washed out the casserole, scouring off the rim and the lid. Put back into the clean dish it looked more palatable if seriously diminished. He dribbled in some water, shook pepper and salt, tasted it. It was very watery. Perhaps he should mix up some flour and water? Guessed there probably wasn't time, it would have to do. He took the basin with the burnt bits out to his car, he could dispose of it when he did the sausages.

Coming back in from the fresh air he realised there was still a strong smell, perhaps if he made some coffee it might help? He made two mugs, put one in the oven and walked around the kitchen with the other dispersing the aroma.

They were back before he could make his getaway.

'You still here, Thomson?' Mother-in-law asked.

'I thought I'd wait and see how Percy got on'.

Mother-in-law was peering into the casserole, 'Goodness its reduced more than I thought, you did take it out at half-past Thomson?'

'Yes, it must be cold by now, well I'll be getting on'.

'Oh, I'd like you to stay, the garden needs finishing off, I'll make you a salad for your lunch.

The steak-and-ale-pie was a blur in the distance.

Next morning Maria answered the phone, 'It's Mother', she said, 'she wants to know why there's a mug of coffee in the oven Thomson?

Bucket and Spade

She looked at the money on the table set neatly beside the tickets. A day at the seaside for the boy he'd said, goodness knows he gets little enough, and make him keep on his tee-shirt if anyone sees those bruises you'll be in trouble.

It wasn't fair, Martin saying that, she hadn't touched the boy, that was Carl's doing and she'd given him the elbow pretty smartish when she'd found out. No-one gives me any credit, she thought, I do my best. She knew the money and the tickets were Martin's way of saying goodbye, but what the heck, like the proverbial there'd always be another one along.

It wasn't her idea going to the beach but perhaps it wouldn't be too bad, after all the kid was nearly five, old enough to be left while she had a drink, it was promising to be very hot, she'd need a drink. Mind you buy him a bucket and spade, Martin had said, and chips, make it a nice day for him.

The train was very crowded, he had to sit on his mother's lap, it wasn't very comfortable, they were both too thin for comfort. The noise and the crowds scared him, he hoped he wouldn't be sick, it always annoyed her.

When they got off the train the sharp smell of the sea reached him, he felt the first tentative shiver of anticipation, trotted more easily by her side. On the promenade she asked him what colour bucket and spade he wanted and he said unhesitatingly 'lellow'. She laughed, one day, she said, you'll say that properly, and added some crisps and a small bottle of lemonade to the purchases.

He clutched her hand when they stepped onto the beach, wary of the soft sand under his feet. She spread a towel near the tide line, so he could make sandcastles with the firmer sand, and he sat solemnly on it, clutching his bucket and spade.

For heaven's sake, she said, play with the sand, I'm just going up to the shops, whatever you do, don't move from the towel and keep your tee-shirt on or you'll get sunstroke. I won't be long, remember, don't move from the towel.

She made her way unerringly to the nearest bar, sank gratefully onto a stool, (more chance of a free drink at the bar). She'd just have one drink, no-one could begrudge her that, the kid would be alright, he would never disobey her. Martin always said he was too quiet by half, not like her, she liked a good time, after all she'd say, we may be dead tomorrow. She'd just have one more, then get back, felt quite virtuous at the thought. Someone offered her another.

Outside the sky was darkening, thunder in the air. The heat and the noise had made the boy feel sick, for a while he lay down on the towel and slept, then woke frightened and thirsty, the lemonade had long been drunk. He wondered if his mother would be much longer, perhaps she wouldn't be able to find him. It was then that he saw the sea, that seemed so far away was coming nearer. He knew nothing of tides, couldn't understand how it kept coming forward and back, but each time a little further forward, would it come to where he was? Would it cover the whole beach? With mounting terror, he watched it until all too soon it licked the edge of his towel.

Frantically he pulled it back, forgetting his bucket and spade which floated away on a receding wavelet.

He stood up, reaching out for them, then the sickness rose in him and the sun and the sea and the sky whirled about his head.

The first thunder spots were falling as she came out of the pub, she was surprised to see how dark the sky was. The clap of thunder partly sobered her, she remembered the boy and tried to push her way through the crowds streaming up from the beach. He'd be alright, she knew, he'd be sitting there on the towel. Looking over the deserted beach she saw the towel lazily curling and uncurling at the water's edge, beyond it the yellow bucket and spade bobbed on the water.

The rain was heavy now, lightning slashed the dark clouds, she stepped into the water, he'd be there somewhere, he wouldn't abandon his bucket and spade, she just had to go far enough, then she'd find him. She stumbled. Fell, vomited up seawater along with some of the drink. She forgot for a moment why she was there, was lost in a curtain of rain, confused and disorientated. The boy, she must find the boy, she knew he was here somewhere, staggered on, felt the buoyancy of the deeper water and unresisting, let the tide take her.

He waited a long time for her to come. First at the hospital and afterwards at the children's home.

They told him she was dead, but he didn't believe them, he knew she was punishing him for losing his bucket and spade.

Under the Bed

I get very nervous when I go to bed now, no longer have I the luxury of settling down for half-an-hour's read with a mug of cocoa. When I do nod off it's to horrendous nightmares, I'm chased, mangled, consumed.

It all began when I fell out with Housework. Funny how I didn't see it coming, how I could have been deceived for so long. Not that it was ever a great passion, no way was I going to clutch Mr Sheen to my bosom, just a really steady relationship, a coming together at certain times to do what had to be done. With respect and a sort of shy affection.

I began to have doubts, I suppose I was naïve really, not realising it sooner, I bet there's lots of you haven't twigged it yet, the plain truth is, housework never stays done!

It all unravels behind your back, does the kitchen floor stay clean, the dust stay off the mantelpiece? In your dreams!

So anyway, we had this enormous row, that's it, I said, you're on your own now, I don't want anything more to do with you. It sniffed a bit and waved a duster in my face, but I was adamant, you've conned me all those years, I said, when its always been my ambition to be a slut.

Those first heady days were wonderful, I was free to sink into chaos. Down to the bottom I went, singing all the way. When the sink was full of dishes I ate out, as the telly crusted over with grime I went to the cinema. I learned to kick things out of the way, grew quite fond of the rubbish in the corners. The fact that the room became quite dim with the unwashed windows was a boon, so much kinder to my complexion.

I was truly in love with my life when I had a call from my Godmother. She was coming to stay, just a few days, darling, in your lovely little house, you keep it so beautifully. Panicking I thought of excuses, a fire perhaps? Or smallpox? But she was fairly ancient and the only one with any money to leave. She always said I was her favourite. I couldn't risk it. I had no choice but to grovel. I suggested to Housework a little armistice. Run getting together again up the flagpole and see if Mr. Hoover salutes it?

I was over a barrel and Housework knew it. I found little smiley faces in the dust on the mantelpiece, the cleaner trundled its way out of the cupboard all by itself. Housework kindly reminded me how to plug it in and handed me a pair of Marigolds. Do you know it all comes back to you, like riding a bike. I'd filled six black bags by lunchtime.

Upstairs I had just enough energy to push the bed back a few inches so that I could get at the beard of dust on the valance. I found an earring, several of those things you stab on the back of them, a pen and a dead spider. Only when I poked the spider with the pen it did a Lazarus and scuttled under the bed.

So now you see why I don't sleep well. Underneath my bed there's a very disgruntled creature. Goodness knows what vital organ I stabbed with the pen. I sense him there plotting, gathering troops, I know they're rallying to the cause, carrying banners....kill, kill!

I shall have to move.

The Egg

It was dark in the egg, just a few slivers of light coming through the holes in the top. Candy felt a trickle of perspiration down her back, the costume was already making her itch. Damn you Brian, she thought, damn you.

Millicent had said much the same thing two days earlier, 'you hadn't mentioned your new PA, Brian, I wouldn't have known anything about it if I hadn't called in the office with that dry-cleaning for you to take home, Miss Paterson on reception had great pleasure telling me all about her, flighty little thing, apparently. Now I know why you've been working late, you can't fool me Brian, and I'm telling you now, I won't have it'.

'Millie love, she's just a secretary, you know I wouldn't play around, I've been working late to get the Easter promotion under way, you know how fussy Derek gets, and there's this chap Adrian come over from head office, currying favour with the boss all the time, it's 'yes Derek I'll do that, Derek' so if there's any extra work to be done I must be the one doing it.'

Only slightly mollified, Millie grumbled, 'I don't know how you can be thinking of Easter this time of year'.

'You should be used to it by now love, after all its what puts the cake on the table'.

And Candy, he thought, puts the icing on the cake for me. True there were occasions when he realised he'd made a mistake, as a secretary she was rubbish, but then again, she never minded staying late, and she flattered him and made him feel young again.

It was when Brian was looking for some props for the promotion that he came across the egg, left over from some long ago advertising stunt. It was very large, and though it was dusty it seemed in reasonable condition. It gave Brian an idea.

'You see Candy,' he explained, 'I've been trying to think of something to surprise Derek with, after the promotion, when we all go back to the boardroom for drinks. We all know Derek likes the old movies, the Follies, and in them there's sometimes a big drum or something and when it's opened a gorgeous girl jumps out, all spangles and feathers. We could use the egg and you could be the girl'.

'Oh, I couldn't, not in front of the boss…could I?'

'Of course, you'd be great'.

There were a lot of practical details to be worked out, he found the egg only opened from the outside, there were segments with cords attached. It was a very fussy egg, all bows and ribbons. He bored several holes in the top, so Candy wouldn't suffocate, though he didn't intend her to be in there for long. He calculated that if he placed the egg in front of the velvet curtains in the boardroom he could stand behind the curtains and pull the cords from there.

He took Candy to the shop that sold fancy dress costumes and hired a suitable dress for her. He had to admit that young as she was she was a far cry from the Hollywood beauties he remembered. But they would have had a few drinks by then and he could dim the lights.

'I'll tap the egg when I'm going to open it, you be ready with a big smile'.

He was perspiring by the time they got back to the boardroom, they'd been downstairs far longer than he'd anticipated.

'Brian', Derek called him over, 'slip downstairs and fetch my briefcase, will you, there's a good chap'.

Brian was furious, he raced down the stairs, was too puffed to race back, took the lift.

It hadn't broken down in all his time with the firm, but it did now, stranding him between floors.

Back in the boardroom things were getting lively, Derek was saying, loudly, 'No I don't know why that stupid egg is there, cover it up somebody, it's getting on my nerves'.

Adrian was the first to take off his jacket and throw it over the top of the egg, then the others all followed and soon the egg was completely covered.

28

'Where the hell's Brian?' Derek asked.

'I'll go and look' said the obliging Adrian.

He could hardly speak for laughing when he got back, 'The lift's stuck, he's between floors, sounds pretty mad.'

It was a huge joke, they carried out their glasses, sat on the floor by the lift gates, sang ribald versions of 'three old ladies' fetched bottles and topped up glasses. During a lull, Derek said, he's trying to tell us something about an egg.'

'You can't have one till Easter' they shouted.

Derek said, 'hush boys, I think he's crying'.

Shredded

This wallpaper will have to go for a start, I can't be doing with roses climbing up trellis work. I need to make a statement here. There's a little loose bit and I pick at it and it runs right down to the skirting boards. I prise a bit more and soon I've cleared a whole patch. This is the most fun I've had in ages.

There's nothing to put the bits in so I kick them into a corner and spread the colour chart on the windowsill. Not a great view, just the back of the pub in the next street. I wonder if they ever empty those bins?

I'll have to decorate this room first, I was thinking of emerald and magenta, but it might bring in the walls a bit. Bijou, the agent said, compact and bijou. That applies to the kitchen too though there is a cooker. At least I think it's a cooker, I shall have to rely on the telly ads....one swipe....

I won't think about the bathroom, mustn't get too depressed.

I've never been one for the do-it-yourself lark, but it can't be too difficult, if I can brush on makeup then surely I can manage walls, same technique, different brush.

First step on the property ladder the agent said, it might seem a step to him, it took a crane to get me this far, had to let the car go but it is within walking distance for work. Just. So, I can tear up the diet sheets, I'll be fit as a fiddle.

Friends have rallied round with offers of furniture, I'm on a firm promise of three coffee tables and a stool and Mandy has finally got her divorce and ended up with a picture of the mother-in-law in costume for the drama group.

She said it would fill the space on my walls till I can afford a Picasso. So, I'm lucky really, I've something to eat off, something to sit on and Mother Courage on the wall. If that isn't making a statement I don't know what is.

Could all have been different of course, if I'd taken the cheque. I'll always remember the bafflement on his face when I tore it up, tore and tore it till it lay between us like the confetti we never got around to.

In all my scullery-maid existence with him I'd never baffled him before. I knew I was knocking into touch a few dreams, the white-dress-and-ring-one, and the charming-young-mother-and-adorable-children-one.

I can see a gang of hoodies outside the pub, they're tipping over the bins.

You know all I came away with was a small bundle of letters he wrote from LA when he went on that business trip. Came back with a fat contract and ....her! I've been taking the letters into work and slipping them through the office shredder. All the dear's and darling's and love-you's chopped up with the whereas's and hereto for's and as of this date's.

I'm wondering how to fill in the holes in the walls where the paper took away some of the plaster, do I fill them in with cement? I'll never get one of those mixers in here.

I must decide on a colour scheme, emerald and magenta isn't going to work.

What the hell, I'll tear up the colour chart, as my auntie always says, you can't beat a nice magnolia.

The Barrier

The hills are quiet this morning, they distance themselves from me. In sorrow, anger? Are the thin shreds of clouds urging the tears I cannot shed? Behind me the cottage is silent, nothing disturbs this terrible stillness, this waiting, the fear.

Over on the ridge the sheep mourn at the grass, move their heavy bodies towards lambing. I shan't see the lambs this year, nor pick the first primroses from the hedges. When the broom makes the hills smile it will be for someone else's eyes.

It was summer when we came here, and the lovely green hills sang that day, they lifted me up, promised me safety and sanity. 'I'll cherish you' Callum said, 'I'll throw the demons over the hills to eternity'. And for a while it was as he promised, but they were just waiting, my demons, if I opened cupboards or doors too quickly, they pounced, if I turned around too sharply they leapt at me.

Sometimes when I became distressed Callum would take me walking in the hills away from the cottage, even there they lurked in the bushes, sprang at me from boulders, the sheep looked at me with evil eyes. He tried so hard, poor Callum, he gave me love and support and pity; sometimes the pity was for himself, and why not? I gave him so little.

He thought everything would be different when the baby came, but often the child would slip from my mind and Callum would come in from the fields and lift her up, wet and screaming and hungry, and then I would be sad and cry over her and he would have to comfort us both.

Sometimes I wondered what it must be like to be Callum, to have the burden of the child and myself. To be my barrier against the world.

Until last night.

A fugitive breeze ruffles the grass at my feet, I shiver and wait, and

32

wipe my bloodstained hands on my dress.

The Wrong Signals

So, home again. The house smells musty, though its only been ten days. I suppose I should unpack but I won't, I've thrown the case into the spare bedroom, there's no way I ever want to see those clothes again.

Heavens! The money I've wasted, I could cry, but I've gone beyond crying, there's a great big lump of anger inside me that'll explode any minute now.

Like everything else in my life, it's my own fault.

I should have known better, life doesn't dish out the sort of goodies I thought were coming my way at last. You have to be pretty special, and I was never special, never the one picked out of the crowd, born to be an extra without any lines to speak, anonymous, the third slave on the left, a blur in the distance.

I'll put the kettle on, have a cuppa, a proper one, funny how foreigners can't make tea. William bought me a cup of tea that day at the church 'do'. And he remembered my name, 'here you are Grace and one for your friend'.

Well Maggie wasn't really my friend, we've been on the same tea rota twice, chatted now and then outside the church, grass needs cutting, terrible weather, that sort of thing. We just happened to be sitting together that day.

Ever so pleasant he was, William, nice suit, tie with red and blue stripes, very clean fingernails. He asked me for a dance, we don't do those modern things, not in the church hall, just a waltz or a foxtrot.

'I haven't seen you here before' I said, 'have you just moved to the village?'. He said he was a cousin of the vicar and happened to be in the neighbourhood on business.

I could see a few eyebrows raised, I'm usually the one collecting teacups or debris in a black plastic bag. William sat with Maggie and me and the vicar and the talk got around to the holidays and the terrible weather we'd been having. William said he was going on a cruise, hoped to get some sun in the Mediterranean.

Maggie said 'I've never been on a cruise' so he told us all about it, the name of the ship and what the food was like, and I said 'Lucky you, I could do with a holiday, can I come too?'

'Wonderful' he said, 'the more the merrier'.

We all laughed, and Maggie said we couldn't go without her and William bought us another cup of tea. His hand sort of brushed mine when he handed me my cup, and afterwards he helped us with the washing up.

It was quite cosy in the kitchen with him and the vicar and Maggie and me. Once I almost slipped on the wet floor and William straightaway put out his hand to steady me. When it was time to go he helped me with my coat and he didn't do that for Maggie.

We said goodbye and I said, 'I mean it, I'll see you on that cruise', and William said, 'I'm looking forward to it'.

I didn't sleep very well that night, I kept going over the conversation and remembering how his hand brushed mine, and how he'd given my shoulder a bit of a squeeze when he helped me put on my coat.

Anyway, to cut a long story short, I wangled the time off work, drew out all I had in the building society, shopped for clothes like I've never shopped before and booked myself on the cruise.

I don't think I've ever been so excited in my life. Booking so late I could only get an inside cabin, it was very small and to be honest it scared the life out of me, being so sort of trapped. When dinner was announced I went out all exhilarated at the thought of seeing William again but then I got lost in all the gangways and things and ended up going back to my cabin and eating a Mars bar I had in my bag.

The next morning, I went out on deck and wandered around until I saw him leaning on the rail. I didn't want to make it too obvious, so I leant on the rail a bit further down, and when I saw him move, I did too, but kept looking out to sea so when we bumped into each other it seemed by accident.

I really think that for one moment he didn't recognise me, he looked totally flummoxed, couldn't remember my name. I said brightly, 'Well I said I'd come, are you pleased to see me?'

I've never seen a man splutter and stammer so much; little specks of spit fell on to my new blouse.

'Yes, of course, we must have a drink one evening'.

So, I'd got it all wrong and then the right signals were coming at me loud and clear.

I had to save face.

'Actually,' I said, 'I'm with some friends, they had a spare ticket, I'd forgotten you were coming on this trip, I might take you up on that drink sometime'.

I saw relief and puzzlement on his face, funny he didn't look so good in shorts and tee-shirt, the smart suit had hidden the paunch.

Did you know they can have storms in the Mediterranean, this one lasted two days and I was so seasick I thought I was going to die.

When I finally tottered out I saw William seated at the bar. With Maggie. I swear his hand brushed hers as he handed her a glass of wine.

The Scream

Thomson carefully carried a small portion of heaven in his hands, the devil had tempted him, and he'd fallen, heavily, gratefully, sublimely.

It had all come about because Maria had insisted Thomson took the train, I know that place well, she'd said, it's not that far from the station, the walk will do you good, set you up for your meeting, you use the car far too much.

The walk, totally underestimated, made him late, he had no time to get anything to eat, and there'd been no trolley on the train, so he spent most of the meeting coughing, trying to disguise the rumblings of his tummy.

After the meeting the chairman had clapped him on the back, 'nasty chest you've got there old man, spot of Vick and an early night eh?'.

Thomson looked in vain for a taxi back to the station, he couldn't risk being late it was dinner at the in-laws that night, which was enough of an ordeal without the shame of being late, so at something approaching a trot he set out.

Past a fish and chip shop.

The smell like all the perfumes of Arabia hit him square on, he was immediately back, pre-marriage, to the halcyon days of bachelorhood, where chips were part of life, chips, sausages, pies…

He stood in the queue, he knew it was going to make him late, he'd have to wait for the next train, if there was one, but nothing could thwart him now, not even the hilarious laughter from the queue when he confidently put down a fifty-pee to pay. Well it had been a long time.

Dazed by the hot little parcel in his hands he took a wrong turning, found himself on a road he didn't remember.

A high wall ran alongside a deserted pavement, not a pedestrian in sight to ask the way, he hoped it was going in the right direction for the station.

The grease was seeping through, he could wait no longer. Putting down his briefcase he went to open paradise. Something born of his marriage, his in-laws, made him pause.

Maria would certainly smell chips on his clothes, his breath, think Thomson think!! What if he took off his jacket, rolled up his sleeves, held the chips well away from himself? Then when he got to the station he could buy a bottle of water, drink, pee, have a wash, and if there was still a whiff he'd say he sat next to someone eating them. Sorted! Careful to balance the precious parcel on his briefcase, he took off his jacket, rolled up his shirt-sleeves, one of his cufflinks dropped on the ground, he'd have to find it later.

The first salt-and-vinegar drenched beauty was halfway to his lips when behind the wall, exactly at his back there was a scream. A real, horrific I'm being murdered scream, nothing like Maria's when she saw a spider or the mother-in-law's screech, 'don't take another step Thomson, there's mud on your shoes'.

Nothing matched this, the chips flew out of his hands, scattered on the pavement. He felt the deepest sense of loss since the hamster died. The one he'd been entrusted to look after for the class.

Silence then, no sound from behind the wall. Tentatively he called, 'hello, are you alright?'. No answer, not even a car went by, there was just the sound of his tummy rumbling, cheated of its sustenance. Dilemma's made up a fair portion of Thomson's life, this was one of a long line. He dithered about what to do, perhaps he should call the police if someone was being murdered. They might even be dead for all he knew, or just needing the kiss of life perhaps, he couldn't just walk away.

He went through the channels. 'Police, please'.

'Can I have your name sir?'.

'That's not relevant, officer, it's just that I heard a scream…

'A scream sir? And where was that?'.

'Well it's on a road that I think leads to the station'.

'and the name of the road sir?'.

'I don't know, I'm a stranger here, I'd just stopped….

'and what made you stop sir?'.

'To tie up my shoelace…..

Thomson looked at his feet, slip-ons, no laces.

'and what is your name sir?'.

'I told you it's not important, I'm reporting a possible crime here, someone could be dying behind this wall, please can you send someone?'.

'Have you looked behind the wall sir?'.

'For heaven's sake it's about ten feet tall'.

'So, we have a high wall on a road with no name, and a scream behind it?'.

'Well you could put it like that…..

'Just stay where you are sir, I'll try to locate you'.

'Oh, I can't stay, I've a train to catch, dinner at the in-laws, (a sudden inspiration) look for some chips on the pavement, someone must have dropped them'.

He was on the train when he remembered the cufflink he'd lost. His wedding gift from Maria, gold, a large M and a smaller T curling coyly round the middle leg. One-offs, easily traceable. He knew he was doomed.

The Thaw

The snow had almost disappeared, just small drifts left on the grass. It had been a surly winter until that sudden whitening, the different light making the world look as if it had changed, but underneath it was the same, she knew it was the same.

She pulled on a sweater and walked to the gate, watching as Neil came back across the field. Buster was charging ahead with the same enthusiasm he'd shown going out. Neil wearing his dark suit, black tie and trainers, letting the dog off the leash as he neared the gate. He looked at his watch, 'shouldn't you be getting ready?' he said, 'the cars will be here in half an hour.

'Oh' she said, 'I'm not going'.

'I might have known' he said, 'it wouldn't be like you to call a truce, even for today'.

In the kitchen he took off his trainers, laid them neatly, side by side on newspaper by the stove. She poured him coffee, held out the mug and followed him upstairs, watching from the doorway as he rooted for shoes. 'Those socks are navy', she said, 'you'd better change them'.

'Damn you' he said, 'damn you'.

'Well she would have been the first to notice, wouldn't she? You'll spoil the day wearing the wrong socks.'

She took black ones from the drawer and tossed them to him. He sat on the bed, pale feet on the blue carpet, no corns or calluses, a lifetime of good shoes. Raising his head, he looked pointedly at her jeans and sweater.

'I want you to be there', he said, 'this is my mother we're burying' his voice rose, 'I don't care how bitchy you are, what evil things you say about her, I don't care if you batter on her coffin, I want you to be there'.

Hysteria filled her ribcage, batter on her coffin indeed? Wear a

40

red suit and a floral hat? Dance up the aisle?

She reached into the wardrobe for her black suit, took out a cream blouse and the black shoes they'd bought in Italy on that last stress-free holiday.

In front of him she stripped, changed underwear, scant black lace, pulled on sheer tights and slashed at her mouth with bright lipstick. He stood up, pulled her to him and kissed her hard, without love. Flicking a tissue, she scrubbed her mouth.

Halfway down the stairs she looked back at him 'The thing is' she said, 'the thing that's really bugging you, you think the wrong one is dead'.

The church was small, unpretentious, one rather good stained-glass window, battered prayer books. White flowers at the altar. Someone should grow black flowers for funerals, she thought, a niche in the market there.

She'd often sidled in at odd hours, when the church was unlocked for the cleaners, or when the good women of the parish came to arrange flowers. Not to pray, not to take comfort from the cross or the piety leaking from the walls but to feel some of the despair easing away. The cold floor, the hard pew, the draught from the door seemed to create a vacuum, a space for just herself. She would watch the busy women at the altar, snipping, selecting, tidying up and wonder about their lives before tiredly slipping back into her own.

Now in the front pew with Neil she heard the muted whispers, the intrusive clack of heels on the stone floor.

One or two people came up and muttered embarrassed condolences, putting tentative hands on his shoulders. She wondered what he was really feeling, poor old piggy in the middle, perhaps she should advertise for a mother for him and had a brief malicious moment wording it. Shamed, she put her hand on his arm and was shocked at the total surprise on his face, as if she was a stranger importuning him.

Deliberately she turned her thoughts to the baked meats, would there be enough, difficult to know how many would come back to the house.

Outside, she felt the chill wind on her legs, envied Neil his trousers and saw with sudden and absolute pity, the traces of tears on his face.

Home then, and that strange post funeral euphoria surged. She poured sherry and urged people to eat. The room filled with talk, someone laughed out loud and looked embarrassed. They began making excuses, long way to go, snow might come back, take care and so on. As much as she hadn't wanted them to come, now she wanted them to stay.

Clearing up and loading the dishwasher took part of the afternoon, Neil of course helped. They made polite small talk, Aunt Lucy a bit frail, did you see Mabel tucking into the sherry? What shall we do with the leftovers?

She knew it was up to her to take them to the next stage. The problem was, could she leave him now?

The ache in her neck and the dryness in her mouth told her she'd fallen asleep in the chair, the television was spitting out its midnight trivia, Neil, she supposed had gone to bed. She'd never fallen asleep like this when his mother was there, all those tense and fraught evenings outside the cosy twosome. Hand washing dishes, tidying tidy cupboards, anything to keep in the kitchen.

She let Buster out, it was cold, clear, no sign of snow, so they needn't have gone so early. Too tired to make a drink, she sipped some water and put out the lights. Outside their bedroom door she hesitated, would he be awake?

The room was empty, the bed untouched. Sketchily, she washed, brushed her teeth, put on her nightdress.

'Oh God, surely he wasn't in her room?

The ghost of his mother's perfume reached her. No sleeping Neil, no weeping Neil. Just forlorn bags of clothes for the charity shop. She thought of all the shopping, the choosing and buying, the tweaking in front of the mirrors, does this suit me, can I take this colour?

Cautiously she opened the spare room door, wondered how one could always tell when a room was occupied.

'I'm not asleep', his voice came out of the darkness.

She was aware how the landing light would be silhouetting her and shivered a little.

'Are you alright'? she asked.

'I don't know, it's been a difficult day'.

A day to be got over, a day to acknowledge the drawn line. 'Why did you come in here? she asked.

'You looked so tired and I thought you might not want....'

All the times she'd wanted to be alone, when they'd lain isolated in the same bed, because she wouldn't give his mother that small victory. Was it what she wanted now?

The question receded, she was very tired.

'I appreciate all you've done today, he said, 'I know it wasn't easy'.

'Yesterday' she said, 'it was yesterday'.

She came into the room and sat on the bed, he eased his legs away to give her room. She saw his face against the pillow, one arm raised so that the thin fingers touched his brow.

'Headache? she said, from habit.

'I don't want you to leave', he said, 'I know you've been thinking about it'. All the choices patterned themselves around her.... leave, stay, continue the feud? She thought about the bags of clothes, the stale perfume, the sad debris and clutter of lives. What was important and what was not. She took his hand, kissed him briefly.

'I'll stay' she said.

Selwyn's last Ride

We were always true to our traditions in the valleys, true to our choirs and chapels, our gossip and scandals. Hardly a man who hadn't sung Messiah, hardly a woman who hadn't spread the rumour, true or false. You have to make do with whatever comes your way in close communities like ours.

I had a cousin who came to stay once, from over there in England. 'It's a bit bleak isn't it?' he said. 'Bleak?' I said, 'It's lovely, bloody lovely, look at them black hills and the little houses flying up the road and the old wheel where the colliery was'.

He didn't stay long, 'Insular' he said, 'that's what you are'. I asked our Malcom what it meant, he said 'I think it means you don't go out much, our Dad'.

Not very bright is Malcolm, takes after his mother. She agrees mind, says she couldn't have been all there to marry me. She used to worry about Malcolm, didn't want him to go down the pit like me. There's no pit to go down now and to tell the truth some of us would like to see it back, good money it was, the last few years and nothing now to take its place.

Left its little legacy of course, the coughing and the black lungs but there, that's life, or death, as the case might be, which it very often was. We quite liked funerals, in the valleys, other peoples of course, we enjoyed a good cry, we felt we had the right pitch for it, what with all the practice.

It was a funeral that gave us a good laugh, and we still chuckle about it.

Since I was a nipper old Selwyn Jones kept the drapers in the High

Street.

Business had been going down for years, he was never going to shift the last of those liberty bodices, though our Mam said you couldn't beat him for knicker elastic. So old Selwyn put the shop up for sale and took himself off down to Cardiff for a little holiday with his sister.

Well, he wasn't there a week when he had a heart attack and died. The old gossips had a field day outside the post office, some said his sister had poisoned him and others thought it was the fast life and the nightclubs.

After choir practice on Friday night, Owen Parry, our conductor, got a few of us together to see how many were going to the funeral. Selwyn had always given us a bit of a discount on our shirts for the Eisteddfod and no one liked the thought of him having no friends to see him on his way. His sister had him in a posh funeral home in Cardiff, which was something we weren't used to, as we always put our dead in the parlour.

Without coming to blows we decided who was going, and Harry who sang tenor with me, said he'd take me in his car, well, mine wouldn't have got us past Ponty. Some of the wives were tagging along because they wanted to see what Selwyn's sister's house was like, her having money and all.

The funeral home was all flowers and soft organ music and no body spoke above a whisper. We felt right shabby in our old serge, but even so we wouldn't have changed places with Selwyn. It comes over you in places like that that as long as you've two legs to carry you out, you're laughing.

After the service the women went back to get the ham salad on the go and we went to bury the corpse.

Now all Selwyn's relatives were buried in the cemetery at Tredegar, family plot or something, so we had a nice little ride ahead of us. Fair play, his sister had laid on cars, lovely grey Silver Clouds. Harry and me and a couple of the others were in the second car, with our posh chauffeur in his grey uniform. We felt like lords, it was like riding on silk. We had a job trying to keep our faces looking solemn.

In one of the little towns I saw a man take off his hat and stand to attention, very respectful. He was a few yards down the road when I saw him the second time and coming out of the bank, the third. It was then we realised we were going around in circles. We could only hope people thought the tears running down our cheeks were from grief.

The hearse stopped, and the driver got out, 'anyone know the way from here' he shouted. Of course, everyone started giving him different directions, in the end Harry shouted the loudest and he got into the hearse alongside the driver. We set off, feeling the joke had worn a bit thin by now and presently the hearse turned into a road going uphill and we wondered why all the cars coming the other way were hooting at us. It dawned on us after a bit that we were going up a one-way street. By this time the road behind us was packed with cars following our lead. It took ages before the mess was sorted out so by the time we got to the cemetery the gates were closed and the vicar had gone home to his tea. When he was fetched he seemed to have very little brotherly love for us and old Selwyn was despatched with such speed we were barely out of the cars. It was a pity life in the drapery trade had left Selwyn with little sense of humour, we on the other hand found the whole thing hilarious.

Finally, we got back to his sister's house where the women had been in touch with the funeral home, the police and finally the Samaritans.

They'd brewed so much tea they'd had to send out for more teabags. My wife drew me to one side, 'How did you get lost?' she hissed, 'you knew the way, you were born in Tredegar, you could have

46

directed them'.

'What! And spoil all the fun?' I said.

Man Flu

You are the light of my life he said, the absolute light of my life.

She didn't think it was much of a compliment, he was fitting a low-energy bulb at the time.

She thought he was more like a candle, tall, vaguely romantic, and extremely susceptible to draughts.

It was a draught that sent him to bed with the sniffles/pneumonia. Dutifully she ran upstairs with drinks and grapes and books and was easily persuaded to sleep in the spare bedroom because if she caught his sniffles/pneumonia she wouldn't be able to run upstairs with drinks and books and grapes.

She quite liked the spare bedroom, she could read till the small hours, drink cocoa and eat buttered toast and to hell with the crumbs.

Came the day when he ventured downstairs, he lay on the sofa with blankets and pillows; easier now to bring him grapes and books and drinks. He became interested in the auctions on the television, made her rootle in the attic for cracked jugs and spoutless teapots. She lined them up on the mantelpiece, it looked like the bottom shelf of the charity shop.

The day he went back to work she threw them out, there was so much junk in the attic he would never know.

He came home exhausted, so much muddle at the office because of his absence, he couldn't face a meal, he'd go straight to bed, she could bring him up some soup perhaps, and scrambled eggs, maybe a bit of the apple tart? He might manage something more substantial later on.

At the foot of the stairs he put his hand on her arm, you have been a brick, he said, an absolute brick, I could never have struggled through this without you, put a bit of cream on the apple tart, would you?

A brick? Had she progressed in the space of a week from a low

energy bulb into a brick?
She liked the sound of a brick.
A brick had weight.
A brick could be thrown.
It could really hurt somebody.
Definitely.

The Losing Day

Numb and obedient she sat in reception aware she was being watched because they'd been anxious someone was taking her home, and she'd lied and said yes, I'm being picked up so now she couldn't use the phone and call a taxi because then they'd know she'd lied and she really wasn't up to the muddle of it all.

It didn't help that it was her birthday, twenty-nine years old and still capable of getting herself into this sort of mess.

She couldn't stay there for ever, so when a car pulled into the forecourt she got up and waved to the receptionist as if to say, 'they're here'.

Outside it felt as if her feet weren't touching the ground, in the space of a few hours the world had changed, she hardly remembered the way to go, buildings wavered, unbalanced her, energy had to be concentrated on putting one foot in front of the other.

In the High Street, shamed by accusing eyes she staggered, completely aware for the first time of what she had done. Blindly she turned into the nearest shop.

Rails of suits, shelves of shirts, sweaters neat on a table.

A suit detached itself, came forward.

'Can I help you'?

'Yes,' she said. 'Oh yes.' She put her hand over her mouth to stifle the words. 'Please put your arms around me, let me cry and cry on your dandruffy shoulders'.

'Were you looking for something?'

'Oblivion,' she wailed, 'I'm looking for oblivion'.

Alarmed, the suit backed away.

'It's a make,' she babbled, 'a make of tie'.

'I don't think' he said frowning, 'is it silk? These are silk'.

He twirled a rack.

'Oh no,' she said eyeing a price tag, 'not silk, I never buy him silk,

50

you see he travels a lot, stays in hotels and then he's so anxious to get home he forgets his ties so if they're silk it gets a bit expensive'.

She thought she would quite like this mythical husband, the travelling highflier, so anxious to get back to her he would leave his ties behind. She saw herself packing his shirts into leather suitcases, accepting his gifts, he wouldn't leave those behind.

The suit led her to another stand.

'Perhaps these might be more what you want'.

He fanned them out sober ones and bright ones, striped and patterned, she felt dizzy, needed desperately to get out of the shop.

'What about that one?'

He mistook her choice, held up a hideous green with little black smudges.

'They're little hippopotamuses' he said, his anxiety palpable, should he have said hippopotami?

'Alright', she said, 'that will amuse him'. Because he would definitely have a sense of humour, this lovely almost-husband, not like that last rat, the ad definitely said GSOH, well she supposed he was laughing now, wherever he might be.

The tie looked even more ghastly away from the rest.

'Do you mind if I give you my change, it weighs the purse down so?'

She tipped it onto the counter, he sighed and counted, pushed a twenty-piece back to her. It looked solitary, abandoned, in her purse, so she took it out and slotted it into the charity box on the counter, hoped it would be happy. Perhaps a pound would take it under its wing, introduce it to the others, this is five, here's fifty...welcome to the box old boy, worth two drops of water to an African child.

In the street she wanted to weep at the thought of the long walk home. Bloody fool, in more ways than the obvious, clutching that dreadful tie that she would be ashamed to give to a charity shop, and buying it with her scrimped together taxi fare.

It had to be too much to lose, all in one day, far too much, a ba...no a foetus, she must remember that, a phantom husband with a talent for losing ties, her dignity, heavens! That Oblivion! She'd even abandoned the twenty pee, was it even now being bullied by a massed rank of ten p's?

Most of all she feared she'd lost for ever her GSOH.

A Round Thingy

Sir Guy was not a happy man, it was probably true to say he was the least happy man in the whole of his little kingdom, give or take the odd beggar or two. So, when his son-in-law Peter put a proposition to him he welcomed it with open arms. He'd never have thought of it himself, at best his mind was a sluggish affair, light years away from anything approaching animation. And as for knowing what year it was, well what did that have to do with the price of parsnips?

A celebration, Peter said, something to mark the occasion, something people would come from all over to see.

A round thingy, down by the river, with things in it.

The more Sir Guy thought about it, the more he liked it, his popularity could do with a boost, that last tax on hay hadn't gone down too well.

Stands to reason, they said in the taverns, puts the price of everything up, can't deliver goods without a cart, you can't pull a cart without a horse and what does a horse run on? Hay!

Sir Guy desperately needed all the groats he could lay his hands on, saddled as he was with fifteen daughters, several of them unmarried. His wife, the Lady Miranda, was no help having retired long ago with a permanent headache.

The daughters still at home led him a merry dance, always borrowing the family cart to go carousing with the most insalubrious peasants.

So, the proposal of a round thingy down by the river topped with a statue of himself and generating a possible supply of endless groats seemed the ideal solution.

The peasants, revolting as usual, were totally against it, if there's any spare groats floating around, they said, then build us some better wells, lower the taxes, forget about a thingy by the river, we'll settle for a mug, even if its got your picture on it.

A Round Thingy

Such a boring lot, thought Sir Guy, no get up and go.

Getting the thing erected was another matter entirely, the builders were always sloping off to do groat in hand jobs in other villages, the wrong sort of clay was delivered, and nobody had any idea what to put in the thing. So far, they had a tatty tapestry, some bones of unknown provenance, and a clay model of a cow where you walked in one end and out the other. A couple of boys practised cartwheels to give a bit of visual entertainment. The village blacksmith eventually proffered a genuine Viking sword he'd knocked up from some metal he had lying around.

Two groats seemed a fair admission price, but considering the average peasant could get through the whole thing in just under a minute, even allowing for them to fall over the cart wheeling boys, Sir Guy reluctantly agreed to charge half a groat with a free carrot thrown in.

Another problem Sir Guy had was the statue, the one of himself that would grace the top of the round thingy.

'It's not my nose 'Sir Guy complained to Owen the sculptor.

'Course its not, yours in on your face, but its as near as dammit'.

As near as dammit wasn't good enough, Owen was ordered to get it right or his bones would be added to the exhibits.

Of course, Owen wasn't really a sculptor, he just happened to have done a couple of gargoyles for the church. Carbuncles they'd been called by a visiting royal.

Owen chipped away at the nose, a bit here a sliver there, until his enthusiasm carried him too far and the nose was reduced to a mere skeleton, a stick insect of a nose, an insult to any decent handkerchief. Too late he realised what he had done, closed the door and took himself off to the tavern.

Several draughts later he went home and took another look at his handiwork. Now that he couldn't focus properly it didn't look as bad as he'd thought. 'Sno so bad' he said, 'just pad it out a bit'. He mixed up some of the chippings with water and drunk, made a better job than if he'd been sober. He went to bed a relatively happy man.

In the morning he could see that because of the water the nose was several shades paler than the rest of the face. It looked ghastly, anaemic, an affront to its owner's bibulous habits.

Bit of paint'll touch it up, he thought, pity it's gone a bit baggy at the end, sort of settled into a different shape.

Colour blindness is a funny thing, a serious obstacle when it comes to painting.

Meanwhile back at the ranch, as they say, Sir Guy was hosting a meeting with the local soothsayers, they were anxious to remind him that the end of that particular year marked the end of the world. They wore sackcloth and ashes and beat their breasts with puny fists.

'Repent, repent' they cried, the dust flying from the sackcloth, 'woe, woe!'.

Peter burst in just as Sir Guy was shooing them away, 'Quick, quick', he cried, 'they're putting your statue on the round thingy'.

Sir Guy pulled on his robe, after all this was his moment of fame. The people made way for him as the statue was hauled into place.

Behind him the laughter of the peasants was generous, it swelled into a crescendo, wave after wave soaring joyously over his head, over the statue with its big red nose.

One of the soothsayers became very agitated, 'I've seen that' she shouted, 'in a vision, everyone wearing big red noses'.

Even as he spoke the weight of the statue became too much for the flimsy roof of the round thingy, slowly and majestically it disappeared.

There was a stunned silence, Peter took the distraught Sir Guy aside.

'Not to worry', he said, 'They've sent a message down from the Priory, the Millennium isn't till next year'.

Possibilities

The clatter of the crows wakes me, they burst from the trees as the car comes up the road. Not that I was really asleep, I'm never really asleep, and normally I like the crows, they're company, and if I squint my eyes their nests look like sheet music. I while away the time trying to make a tune from them.

It's been quiet here for so long the car is an intrusion, though not without possibilities, there are always possibilities. I'll stay up here and see what happens. The thing is, this road doesn't lead anywhere, its marked down at the Pike, no through road. So the car must mean to come here, unless of course the driver is illiterate, or stupid.

It stops, facing the front of the house. For a moment the passengers sit there. The 'For Sale' board has long since abandoned hope, it lies in the weeds and has to be stepped over to get to the gate.

A man in a suit eventually gets out, followed by another all smart/casual (see I keep up with the jargon). His partner veers towards the Marks and Spencer traditional, she shudders when she sees the crow's nests. Nineteen all told, I've counted them.

Already she is bleating, 'George you can't be serious, this is miles from anywhere!'.

But George is already following the agent into the house, they don't have to step over any junk mail, not since I frightened the postman off, must be two years ago now, I really should keep a calendar.

George has pounced on the little room off the hallway, I sit in there sometimes, it gets the morning sun. If you can call it sitting.

Look Marjorie, this is perfect for my study, I can get on with my book, all the peace and quiet I need, and this place is big enough for you to have your family over, well, some of them, I don't think your Mother would like it.

He turns to the agent. 'Four bedrooms'?

The agent nods, leads the way. On the stairs Marjorie shivers, 'Oh, someone walked over my grave'.

Not yet my darling I think, but soon.

I move ahead as they peer into rooms. The bathroom partly mollifies Marjorie. It's state of the art, (more jargon!) and very mirrored, which is why I don't go in there. The previous tenants put it in before the tragedy. I remember her saying, 'We'll start up here Justin, work our way down'. I snigger about it sometimes, because that's what she did, worked her way down. Headfirst.

Marjorie is still twittering on in spite of the bathroom. 'Please George, let's go, I don't like this place at all'.

He brushes her off, I can tell he's regretting his earlier enthusiasm to the agent. Starts to find fault, kitchen needs work, fourth bedroom too small, is that damp on the kitchen ceiling?

The agent says its mostly cosmetic, as if a swipe of moisturiser is all that's needed. He isn't worried, he knows George is hooked.

George is all nonchalance, well, if we were interested, price is way too high. They go into a huddle, Marjorie steps back, this is man's work. She gazes sadly at the crow's nests, she knows she's lost this battle, the crows are hers now.

The agent says he'll take George's offer back to the client and give him a ring.

George betrays himself by giving his phone number, his mobile, Marjorie's mobile, the neighbour's.

They drive off, so new tenants hey! Wonder what I can do with them, too risky to do the stairs again, perhaps something electrical? Marjorie looks as if she wouldn't be too much trouble. Appliance in the bath maybe? As long as George's fingerprints are on it. Or does the water wash them off? I'm going to be a busy little bee researching this.

I was the first victim of course, the old pillow over the face, but they did catch him, and they caught Justin too. Soon, fingers crossed they'll have George.

It's not revenge, its justice.

A Twiggy thing from Harrods

It was at the bottom, in the thick and secret places, that the rumours started. For a day they circled, gathering strength, confirming, denying, piecing together scraps of conversation. Creating apprehension at the way conjecture was turning into reality.

Spiralling, drifting upwards into the sparser regions where the branches were thin and short. Past the rustling needles, the lights, the baubles, tangling with tinsel, until they reached the top. Until they reached Doll.

No appendage could be added to her name, not in her hearing. She might be dressed in gauze, but inside a different Doll struggled to be let out. She wanted jeans, a mobile, Jimmy Choo shoes, something flighty from Prada, butterfly tattoo somewhere daring.

If the rumours were true, it could only mean one thing….redundancy!

It seemed the lady of the house had seen a twiggy thing in Harrods, hung with crystal pendants. Not a bauble in sight, not the merest shred of tinsel, and definitely no Doll.

She was so angry at the thought of bring cast aside after the years of patient endurance with a fairy light strapped to her back, not to mention the long months in the attic. No chance of her dream coming true now.

And the question loomed, where would they go, charity shop or the bin?

Over on top of the piano the cotton-wool Santa leered at Doll. Angrily she pulled at her skirt, knowing that from her lofty perch he could probably see more than she thought decent. Her greatest pleasure on Christmas Day was seeing his head pulled off while they rummaged inside him for little presents.

She kicked her heels at the tree and needles showered down onto the presents.

So, Christmas passed, and they were all deemed too shabby for Oxfam.

In the bin Doll eased her shoulders away from a clutch of used teabags, snuggled gratefully into something soft and warm.

'Hello' said the snowman, 'do you come here often?'.

Adding Up and Taking Away

The conviction had been growing inside him all morning, he looked over at Meg.

'I have to go back love, I have to say goodbye'.

Meg, wrestling to get one more book into the packing case, swore softly. If Will thought this was the time for jokes, with the final packing to be done and the boys off saying the endless goodbyes instead of helping, then he shouldn't have started all this.

Until now she felt she had coped well with this projected move to America, selling the house, packing up, had looked forward to the new life, better weather, better prospects for Will. Of course, the boys had been against it at first, but then it became cool to say, yeah, we're off to the States and brag about having their own swimming pool.

Just three days to go, with all the last-minute things harrying her, Will's mood she could do without. She looked over at him, he had the look she'd seen before, the air of sadness that certain anniversaries brought. She dropped the book, it wasn't going in anyway, put her arms around him.

'You go love, if that's what you want, it's a long way though, you'll need a day. Best go early in the morning, that'll leave us a full day before we fly, and have a word with the boys, they must do their share. And promise you'll stop for meals'.

It was raining when he set out, the motorway hideous with lorries, often travelling companionably together. All morning it kept up until, weary of the spray and the stupidity of other drivers, he turned into a service station. He had a sandwich, drank some bitter coffee, used the loos and went on his way.

It wasn't until he was over the border that the rain lessened, became the rain of his childhood. Soft, misty, Welsh. Were the hills really greener, was this the other side of the fence, and would he ever feel this way about California?

60

Above the valley he stopped the car. No rain now, soft blue between the clouds. The hillside was green, smooth, untroubled. He had an hysterical urge to roll down the slope, over and over, let the momentum take him down, down to where he'd last seen Carrie.

Cycling down Moy Road, on her way to Pant Glas school. He'd been waiting on the other side of the road for his lift to work. She'd waved, the cycle wobbling, all the love in the world electrifying the air between them. Such a vivid memory though for the life of him he couldn't remember what the weather was like.

It had been warm in her mother's kitchen the day Carrie took him home for the first time. It was always hot in valley kitchens, the fire halfway up the chimney, the coal the perk, the scrap of thanks.

'Mam' she'd said, 'this is Will'.

He'd seen the look in Megan's eyes, the acknowledgement that this was change, the first loosening of ties. Since Dai's black lungs had taken him into that final lowering into the black earth, it had been just Carrie and herself. Now there was Will. As he looked down the valley, he thought back to the two years he'd worked down the pit, hating every minute, the smell of the coal, the plunging cage. Then the blessed chance of a job in the colliery office. Coming up, still tasting the coal but getting cleaner, breathing properly again.

He arrived home one day and heard laughter, his sister Bella with another teacher from Pant Glas.

'This is Carrie' she said.

She had all the sparkiness and sweetness of the valley girls, everything about her fresh and clean. He walked her home that evening, it was the beginning, the start that led to him standing in Megan's kitchen hearing her say, 'Mam, this is Will'.

Someone in the office noticed his aptitude for figures, why don't you study, they said, accountants get good money. So he enrolled in night school, felt a belated drive to aim for something. It was hard, the exams were torture.

Often he had to stay in, to prepare work. Carrie called those times his 'adding up and taking away' times. Adding up for our future, he said, the good job, the nice house, our children. He loved the way she

61

smiled when he said children.

He bought her a ring, two pounds five shillings in Moiseys jewellers in Pontypridd. Promised her a better one when he was qualified. Carrie said she didn't want another ring, this was the one she would wear all her life.

The day he passed his final exams they celebrated with Bella and their friends in the town's café. Now we can get married, Will said.

He still had his job in the colliery office, Carrie had her teacher's salary, they could afford to rent a house. Carrie wanted a Christmas wedding, she was full of plans. Megan of course, would make her dress.

One Saturday in September she and Carrie took the train down to Cardiff, they sat at the table in Howell's the posh shop in St. Mary's Street, looking through the pattern books. Flicking through the styles, this neckline, those sleeves? Lace trimming? Tossing ideas between them, loving every minute.

The pattern chosen, then the white satin, Megan anxiously checking, making sure they had the right amount.

Afterwards they treated themselves to tea in the store's restaurant. Carrie liked Cardiff, wondered if this was where Will would work, pictured them in a nice house in the suburbs.

Back home Megan wrapped the satin in a clean sheet. Carrie was impatient for her to start it.

'It's half term soon could we do it then?'.

Megan looked at the photograph of herself and Dai on their wedding day in pride of place on the mantelpiece.

She thought how he would have liked Will and grieved that he wouldn't be there to give Carrie away. Angrily she stabbed at the fire with the poker. Bloody coal, bloody coal. The sparks flew up, taunting her.

Carrie's cycle flew down the road that Friday in October, seeing Will, waving madly as if the sight of him took her worlds into the sun. Thinking of the coming week, the white satin spread on the table, Megan twisting the pattern this way and that, then the sharp scissors biting into the fabric.

She stood in front of her class, the children's faces turned towards her and she touched the ring on her finger, the one she would wear all her life.

The noise started, coming towards them, as if the largest express train in the world was rolling down the mountain. In the school there was silence, a suspension of thought, a vacuum. The noise became unbearable, the last thing she saw was the fear on the children's faces.

Sitting in his car Will felt his hands remembering, how they'd scrabbled at the bricks, the mud and slime. Carrying children out, the lucky ones and the ones who lay limp in his arms, night and day they worked, listening for cries, digging with their hands, trying to organise chaos.

That time was always to be his nightmare. A betrayal if ever he forgot.

In Megan's kitchen he'd watched as she fed white satin to the flames. Bloody coal she wept, bloody coal.

Computer Literate?

Thomson was desperate for some fresh air, he'd spent what seemed like hours huddled over the in-law's computer, trying to sort out a problem. Silly of him to have said, breezily, yeah, I'll have a look at it, probably something simple, soon fix it. Only he couldn't, and he feared he'd probably wiped out a lot of data in his muddled efforts.

Mother-in-law offered to open the window for him, no way was she going to let him off the hook. Not that she had any confidence in Thomson, but computer experts came expensive.

So, he plodded on, the draught from the window cooling his coffee, he wished she wouldn't stand there, watching him. After all he wasn't a complete idiot, he could access games, play Free-cell, sometimes he could even open his e-mail.

Maria now, was a wizard, did all sorts of complicated things with hers, but she was in London, shopping with friends, he'd have to get it fixed before she came back, she'd soon see what a mess he'd made of it.

Father-in-law had joined his wife, they stood at his back as he clicked furiously, the damned cursor like a demented fly. Suddenly the screen went blank. 'Ok' he said, 'it can happen for no reason, just resting, I'll take a turn round the garden, come back to it fresh....

Outside it felt as if the garden was having a turn round him, he couldn't even guess at the damage he'd done, mother-in-law was on all sorts of committees, kept information stored, boasted she had it all at her fingertips. He felt tempted to run, through the garden, down the lane, till he reached the Red Lion, where he could drink himself into oblivion.

Angry voices reached him from the house.... you should never have let him near it.... you know what an idiot he is…bet he's wiped everything out.

The idiot yearned for a forbidden cigarette, he slouched behind the shed, whimpered a bit, remembered with sad melancholy the carefree days at the office where, if he messed up the computer (it had been known) there was always some clever dick to put it right.

If only he could get rid of the in-laws perhaps he could call on somebody to sort the mess he'd made.

His phone rang, Maria, she was going to be late, they'd managed to get seats for a show. So that gave him something of a breather.

A squirrel contemplated him from the edge of the lawn, decided Thomson wasn't good for anything in the way of nuts and disappeared. He or maybe she, gave him the only good idea he'd had all day.

In town there was a rather good restaurant called The Squirrel, not cheap but to a desperate man what's money?

Casually he strolled back into the house, 'Look,' he said 'I'd like to give you both a treat, you've been very good to me, both of you, so I'll book a table for you and you go and enjoy yourselves. Maria isn't going to be back till late, so I'll work on the computer, actually I think I know what the problem is, simple to put right, should have thought of it before.'

Baffled they found themselves getting ready, stepping into the taxi Thomson had ordered, leaving him alone in the house. That thought struck them simultaneously, they almost turned back, but dinner at The Squirrel wasn't to be sneezed at.

For one precious hour Thomson phoned everyone he knew who could be persuaded to help. Finally, he struck gold, a friend of a friend said he'd help.

'What the heck have you done to it', he said, peering at the screen.

'I'll make you a coffee', 'Thomson said, 'and pay for your time of course'.

It was turning out to be an expensive evening what with the in-law's dinner and the taxi. He didn't know how he'd square it with Maria, she kept a tight hold on their finances.

It took ages to get the computer right, in fact Thomson had only just seen the friend of a friend out when the in-laws were back.

'Well did you get it working?' they asked.

Thomson was all nonchalance, 'What? Oh, the computer, yeah, that was a doddle, done in no time. Did you have a nice meal?'.

Mother wants to speak to you, Maria said at breakfast. 'What about?' Thomson spluttered.

'I don't know, Maria said, 'but she sounds very upset, you'd better get over there smartish'.

Thomson didn't want to get over there smartish, in fact he would have preferred the long route via the Outer Hebrides, but Maria said she was coming with him so smartish it had to be.

Mother-in-law and Father-in-law, arms akimbo, confronted them. Mother-in-law released a shaking arm to point an equally shaking finger at the computer screen. At first Thomson felt relief, it was working, there was a picture.

An overweight, be-stubbled man stared at them. There was a voiceover, it sounded foreign.

Father-in-law turned to Thomson. 'You know, there are only two things we can access now, one is a dating agency in Tokyo and the other is advice on euthanasia. Shall I get that printed out for you?!'

'Thank you' said Thomson, 'it might be useful.'

A Good Boy – Sammy

He came home to the smell of burning potatoes and the sight of the knife at Ma's throat. The man's other hand was in Ma's hair tugging her hair back, and for a fugitive moment Sam saw a younger, leaner, Ma.

He made his voice into a whine, 'leave her alone, she don't know nothing'.

The knife slowly, almost casually, drew a thin line of blood on the dark neck, the man's companion was at the dresser, tipping out the drawers, his hands quick and nervous. The stench from the burnt saucepan aggravated the fear in the room, Sam put out the gas and drew the saucepan back. He held up his hands, palms facing the man with the knife.

'Ok, Ok, I didn't know the delivery was for you, I'll get the money, gimme a day...'

All the menace was in the knife as it slowly drew a second line....

'It's in the outside toilet, loose brick halfway up on the left'.

A nod from the one with the knife and the nervous one disappeared, came back with bundle of notes, substantial, stashed for such an emergency. Sam saw the knife wiped on Ma's dress and pocketed.

When they had gone he bathed Ma's neck, made her some tea and threw out the burnt saucepan.

'Where you get that money, Sam? What you been doing?'

'I'm sorry Ma, I made a mistake, but don't worry about it, the thing is we'll have to go away, they'll likely come back'.

He could have kicked himself for taking the risk that led to this, he'd never intended Ma to be mixed up in his dealings. She'd never been any trouble to him, had climbed out of poverty and shame to a certain respectability.

Going off the church with the other women, singing 'Hallelujah'

67

and 'Praise the Lord'. Ma had praised the Lord for Sammy and offered up excuses for his no-good brothers, they didn't have no chance, she confided, no jobs, no nothing, not where we live. Only Carla, Lord, she's been good to me.

Carla had drifted on to the streets, but she was clever and had climbed several rungs of that particular ladder. When Sam was fifteen, and the only one left at home, she had arranged for money to be banked for them every week. She showed Sam how to make out the cheques and draw their rent and living expenses. The cashier looked pale and anaemic beside his beautiful sister. It was that day at the bank that sowed the seeds, the longing for the power of money.

Every morning he would leave the house in paint stained overalls, sandwiches and drinks in a battered hold-all.

'Where you going, dressed like that Sammy? You aint got no job'.

'Don't worry Ma, I know what I'm doing'.

He did too, never kept any of the drugs in the house, with the money he stashed everything in the derelict house next door. Their gardens backed on to an empty warehouse, by slipping over the fence in the dark he couldn't be seen. Everything kept in tin boxes because of the rats.

Each week he made the rounds of the building societies and the banks, they got to know him, the young black boy pulling a few notes out of a tattered pay-packet, never very much, nothing to get suspicious about. The accounts had built up very nicely over the years, though he needed to keep a certain amount in ready cash. He was very careful not to be seen splashing any of it around, had seen too many caught like that. So he'd always worked solo, kept his eyes and ears keen. Until today.

Listen Ma, I must think this out, you go on to church, but whatever you do don't say anything about this, I'll meet you as you come out, and remember not a word!'.

Still shaking, her best scarf around her neck, Ma went.

Sam walked slowly around the block twice, satisfied himself he wasn't being followed and slipped over the fence to retrieve the tin boxes. In the kitchen he drew the curtains and tipped them out. It was serious money.

He knew he would have to take it with him but was appalled at the risk. He'd been thrown tonight, was outside his own disciplines, though in his heart he'd known this day would come. It was his own fault for being greedy, he could have stopped long ago, had always planned that he would.

He stuffed the money and the building society books into his sports bag, he would have to be extra careful, steer clear of any confrontation.

Outside the church Ma was waiting for him, terrified at the thought of leaving home.

'Where we going, Sam? What we going to do?'

'Don't worry Ma we'll get ourselves a brand-new home, somewhere nice, you'd like a new house now, wouldn't you?'

Ma wanted to go back to the old house, lie down on her bed and shut out the nightmare.

At the train station Sam studied the board, anxious to get away as soon as possible. A train to Manchester was due and he bought single tickets for them.

'I haven't been on a train for oh, must be thirty years, Sam.'

He could see that some part of Ma was beginning to perk up.

Her eyes were lively, and he thought, this is how she could have been, not dragged down by poverty and shame. He was sorry it was dark, he couldn't distract himself by looking out of the window. Ma dozed, came to with a start as they drew into the station.

'Why we come here Sammy?'

He was out of his depth when they left the train, it was quite late, and Ma was tired and cross, wouldn't drink the coffee he'd bought her. For a while they sat on the platform, while he tried to think what to do. They had no luggage and he knew they looked shabby and poor. He got Ma, grumbling, to her feet and they went outside to the taxi rank. Sam asked the driver if he knew somewhere they could stay, he said Ma had been unwell, they'd had to get off the train.

The little hotel was in a back street, the room seemed clean enough though, and Ma lay down on the bed in her slip and was soon asleep.

69

Sam slept with the bag in the bed with him. The next morning, before Ma was awake he took some money out, they would need food and some clothes, though he still had no idea what they were going to do.

They left the hotel after breakfast, Ma was slow and still tired, though Sam was jumpy with impatience. He couldn't understand why it all seemed so difficult, he'd always thought just having money would open all doors. He was careful not to buy too much in any one store, a coat for Ma in one, a dress in another. He sent her into a chain store to buy a nightdress and underclothes. Ma was beginning to look perky again, she'd never spent so much money on herself before. Sam bought a case, choosing a shop-soiled one, getting it cheap. They were both glad to find a café for lunch.

While they were waiting for service, Sam opened the case and put their shopping in it.

'Going on holiday?' said the waitress.

'Yeah'

'Spain', Sam said the first thing that came into his head.

'Lucky you' she was as dark as he was, warm and friendly.

Perhaps this was a sign, his random remark could be the answer, short term anyway, they could sit in the sun and he'd be able to sort things out, and it would give Ma her first real holiday. He would have to do something about the house too, let the landlord know, and Ma's friends would be wondering where she was, make enquiries, go to the police perhaps. He was stupid not to have worked things out more, all the years of being careful and now he'd possibly done the worst thing of all, running away. He wondered too, about the money from Carla, in his ignorance he imagined the bank getting in touch with her.

He took Ma to a cinema, where she sat contentedly with a bumper-sized carton of popcorn. Sam closed his eyes, hoping in the darkness he could come up with some plans, but incredibly he dozed, came to when the lights went up.

'You missed a good picture there, Sammy,' Ma said, putting the empty carton under the seat.

They went back to the café for tea, the girl came forward, recognising them, smiling, on an impulse Sam said, 'Do you know of a small hotel where we could stay for a few nights, there's been a mix up with our tickets, we can't fly till next week.'

'Oh, what a shame, you must be so disappointed, there's quite a few places near here, I'll show you the way when you leave'.

Ma drank her tea, bit into a chocolate éclair.

'You been telling an awful lot of lies, Sammy, you know we aint going to Spain, and where you get all this money, you'll end up in jail like your brothers.'

'Keep your voice down Ma, I'm looking out for you aren't I? none of the others 'cept Carla gave a toss whether you lived or died. Perhaps we will go to Spain, have a holiday and when we come back we'll look for a nice little house, near here perhaps, where you can go to church and sing 'Praise the Lord.'

'I praised the Lord, Sammy, but I don't think He'll listen any more'.

Sam paid the bill and the girl came over and stood on the pavement with them, pointing the way. She put her hand on Sam's arm as she gestured, straight down, first left, second right.

He daydreamed as they walked, pictured himself taking the girl home to Ma's nice new house, everything clean and bright and respectable. Perhaps they'd marry, have kids, but no more than two, not a brood like Ma's too many to feed, to control.

The hotel had room for them, two rooms in fact, each with its own bathroom, which Ma thought was ever so posh. Sam locked his door and took out the money, he'd never thought of it as a burden before, but if it wasn't exactly that, it was a serious problem. Perhaps the best way was to stash it away in the various building society accounts. At least it would be safer, the bag was too vulnerable, he couldn't go on for ever clutching it. He separated out so much for each account.

He could hardly stuff his pockets with them he really needed envelopes, mark each one with the name of the building society, mustn't pull out the wrong one. Perhaps Ma could have some in her handbag, he didn't think much would faze Ma now.

He hid the bag under his bed, locked the door and went down to

71

reception. He asked if they could spare him some envelopes, they proffered two small ones, but he said he needed more, so they told him there was a shop that opened late, they'd have some, cut down the lane at the back, it'll be quicker.

He went back to his room, retrieved the bag, afraid to leave it.

As he turned into the lane, the thought came to him that the sensible thing to do was to contact Carla, she would know what to do about the money and she'd see to the landlord and spread the word among Ma's friends that she'd gone on holiday. True, she'd never known of Sam's activities and there might be some sticky questions as to why he had lived off her generosity, but he was sure she'd realise he'd done it all for Ma, so that Ma could live in a nice little house of her own.

Yes, Carla was the answer, he punched the air with satisfaction, pleased with himself, back on course.

Halfway down the lane he was aware of a man detaching himself from the wall, felt the bulk of him as he was slammed against the wall. A hand gripped his throat, he felt the prick of a knife against his ribs. There was just enough light for Sam to recognise the look on the face so close to his own, drug crazed, not to be reasoned with.

Sam dropped his bag fumbled in his pocket for money, the man snarled hoarsely, 'gimme the watch as well, and your jacket, put it in the bag'. Sam's heart sank, 'leave me the bag' he said, 'need it for work'.

There was the sound of running feet and Sam went weak with relief, but it was a mate of the muggers' come to give a hand. Share the loot. He tore off Sam's jacket, shoved it in the bag. From further down the lane came voices, friends calling goodnight, see you soon. Sam opened his mouth to shout for help but found himself suddenly winded, he slumped to the ground, aware that his attackers had left him. He tried to lever himself up, but his hands slipped in a sticky pool, before he could work out what it was, he found the handle of the knife, the blade still deep under his ribs. His mind was a kaleidoscope of images, Ma, the girl, envelopes, tens and twenties, and fifties.

When Ma found Sammy wasn't in his room she wandered diffidently down to reception, peered shyly into the lounge, there was a smell of roasting meat from the kitchens. The girl behind the desk asked if she was looking for her son, explained he had gone to get some envelopes.

Envelopes? Sammy?

She made her bewildered way back to her room, sat at the dressing table. I bet he's gone to see that girl, she thought, the one from the café, she remembered how they'd been talking when she'd gone to the ladies, he must have made a date with her then, he'll be bringing her back for dinner, I'll have to pretend it's a surprise, not say I guessed anything.

Ma felt warm and happy, she pulled a comb through her hair, she'd wear her new dress, they'd sit in the dining room, all posh, just like proper folk. Halleluiah, sang Ma, Praise the Lord.

No-one Clapped

The dandelions are blooming again in the cracks of the flagstones, they form a yellow drift like the one that lined the path on that last walk. There's a little blue flower too, that I don't know the name of, though I remember it grew in the waste ground around our cottage. I didn't know the name of it even then. It seems to me now that I knew all the wrong things, fear and despair, hunger and that last choking panic, but I never knew the names of the birds and the trees. A whole world of knowledge never came my way.

Gunter is at the edge of the field, he is moody today, I don't think he'll stay much longer, I tell him we had no choice in the parts we played, and if we stay to wander the stage like a tardy and unsubstantial epilogue, then so be it. The audience has long since left this particular auditorium, and though the cast was huge it was a very bad play and we had such small parts. At the end, no-one clapped.

Sometimes I go way up high and when I look down this place is so anonymous it blends into the landscape, one can imagine that nothing every happened here. It frightens me that what was once so real can crumble to dust and be blown away.

When the soldiers came we were hiding in the pit our father dug in the barn, our mother surrendered us when she saw their bayonets. We came up into the dusty light of the barn and were herded into carts, father and the boys into one and mother and myself into another. The carts went in different directions. No space, no time for goodbyes, a parting as cold and hard and relentless as the frozen ground we travelled over to the ghetto.

Gunter's life was different, a rural, substantial life. He was used to taking orders from his father and brothers, so army life was tolerable. It was only when he was sent here that some instinct rebelled, he knew that everything that happened here was against nature, against the natural order of things. His anger was submerged,

74

it festered because he could do nothing about it.

Until the end.

We have had visitors today, the first for a very long time, in the beginning they came in droves, reporters, camera crews, politicians. Some of them wept, but tears have always been too gentle for this place. I wanted just one of them to scream, to howl, to come within a fraction of realising what took place here. When they'd gone I saw they had trampled on the little blue flowers.

It was strange in the ghetto, it should have been a place of safety, a refuge, but fear stalked us even there. We had no news of our father and brothers, we were half-starved, the rations of food never satisfying our hunger. Mother gave me some of her share, so she became weak and when a flu epidemic swept the ghetto, she died.

I can see Gunter trying to get a rabbit to eat out of his hand, it sees the grass waved in front of its nose but takes fright and runs away. Few animals ever come here, even the birds stay clear of the sky above us.

There were many others at the burial ground, I wept with them, desolate, not knowing what to do. Someone suggested the orphanage on Sikorsky Street, run by Albie Cohen. I was too old really, but he took me in on condition I helped with the younger children. There was another girl my own age, Mara, and we became friends. Mara was a Romany, dark curling hair, dark eyes, the only survivor of her extensive family.

Together we scavenged for food, dodged the soldiers, talked endlessly as we worked. We talked about boys, love, the life we would lead when it was all over. We had no doubt there was a life for us, out there waiting.

On my birthday, I say to myself, my name is Ilena, I am sixteen years old.

Albie Cohen was a strange man, outwardly unsentimental, his every moment spent in looking after the orphans. He made meals out of the most unlikely scraps, mended clothes, sat up all night with sick children, badgered anyone likely to give food or clothing. Mara and I became his treasured helpers and if it was possible to be happy at such

75

a time, then I was, I had a friend, I had Mara.

I see that last lot of visitors left rubbish behind, the thing is, they don't look back, to them it doesn't matter. When they walk away from here they can pretend it never existed.

The day came when the orphanage was purged. They said Albie could stay, they only wanted to take the children, but he insisted if they went he would too.

It was stifling in the wagons, the young ones cried and clung to us.

At the camp we were recognised for what we were, fifteen-year-old virgins.

I try not to think about it.

It happened. It is over.

Gunter was the guard who fetched us for the officers, his face was a mask and his eyes desolate. He tells me that at the end he shot all the officers he could find until he too was killed. Which is why I tell him not to blame himself, it never was going to have a happy ending.

A few days after my sixteenth birthday Mara and I took that last walk, on the path where the Stars of David floated beside us and where the dandelions now bloom.

Gunter left last night. I shall miss him. Before he went he told me the name of the little blue flower.

Forget-me-not.

As the flowers bloom and die I keep my vigil in this barren place that still echoes with the clamour of the outraged.

My name is Ilena and I am sixteen years old.

Lightning Source UK Ltd.
Milton Keynes UK
UKHW02f1138150618
324247UK00006B/291/P